Allergic

To

Mistletoe

Cynthia Veliz

ISBN: 978-1-7328763-1-6

This book is dedicated to anyone who has

ever fallen in love.

Table of Contents

Chapter One...

Chapter Two..1

Chapter Three...1

Chapter Four..2

Chapter Five...2

Chapter Six..3

Chapter Seven..3

Chapter Eight...4

Chapter Nine...5

Chapter Ten...5

Chapter Eleven..5

Chapter Twelve...6

Chapter One

Opal wasn't sure what was worse, her beautiful turkey being dunked into a giant tub of grease outside or that it was her husband, Luca, who was doing the dunking. Adeleine giggles as she watches her husband Nick and Luca carry the large, stuffed frozen bird outside. She had worked on perfecting the stuffing for the twenty-pound bird for a week and within minutes, it'd be in a large tub of bubbling grease. Opal refills her glass of wine, unsure if she will be able to make it through the event that brought all Bearsville to their front yard without it.

Nick and Adeleine were newlyweds who lived three houses down from Opal and Luca. Except they both had grown up in the snowy mountainside town, while Luca and Opal crash-landed into the snowbank town by accident but ended up falling in love and staying. Opal and Adeleine got along instantly, both smart and driven women. Adeleine was the only accountant in town, putting her degree to good use while Opal kept her eyes peeled for office spaces, she could use to set up her photography studio. While Luca took a while to warm up to the shortsighted Nick, they eventually did form a friendship over an equal infatuation for blueberry pancakes. Unfortunately for Nick, now he was becoming enemy number one to Opal.

"Oh, come on Opal, it'll be fun!" Adeleine grins as she finishes off her fourth glass of wine.

"I somehow doubt that…" Opal sighs as she sets her wine glass down on the butcher block countertop.

Opal grabs her fleece jacket off a nearby dining chair before she follows Adeleine outside. Nick and Luca stand over a large tub of bubbling grease, Opal wasn't too sure of the logistics, she just knew that she was disappointed in her husband for going along with the ludicrous plan.

A few more of their neighbors are drawn in by the scene Luca and Nick are causing, making Opal regret her decision to not fight for her turkey more. Luca says something to Nick and turns and runs towards the house. He's smiling at Opal with that stupid grin, the one that made her anger melt away as soon as she saw it.

"Babe, did you bring the camera?" Luca says as he lifts his foot to hop onto the porch.

Thwack!

7

Opal barely had time to blink as Luca's body slams into the icy covered ground. Opal hasn't even taken the camera out of her pocket when she sees him on the ground. His eyes closed and his previously rapid breathing, now slowed down quite a bit. A bit more than Opal would have liked as she kneels over him. Her hand gently resting on the side of his face.

"Luca?" Opal says looks him over for injuries.

Luca doesn't respond, and no one seems to notice. Adeleine and Nick laugh over the tub of grease as the turkey is slowly lowered into it. Their neighbors cheering them on as Opal carefully tries to rouse Luca.

"Love...come on..." Opal voices nervously, her fingers gently tapping against his cheek.

When Luca still doesn't wake up, Opal pulls her cell phone from her back pocket and quickly dials Joe, the ambulance driver.

Bearsville is so small, that the hospital allows Joe to park the ambulance in his driveway in between emergency calls, as he is only one of two EMT's. The other being an older woman named Rose. Joe answers immediately and arrives only moments later, much to Opal's appeasement.

By the time Joe pulls up, everyone has noticed Luca on the ground. Adeleine's face flushing with worry as she drinks water, trying to magically sober up. Opal tosses her keys to the only person she really trusts, their widowed neighbor, Daria.

Joe and Rose get Luca onto a stretcher, Rose keeping track of Luca's vitals and getting information from Opal on what exactly happened. By the time they reach the hospital, Rose informs Opal that Luca more than likely has a concussion.

Opal's head is spinning as Rose and Joe wheel him into the nearly empty Emergency Department at Bearsville Memorial.

Joe and Rose hand him over to the nurses on staff, who bring him into an isolated glass room and begin to clean up the back of his head, while the doctor comes down. Opal takes a seat on a nearby chair as another nurse comes over to her with a clipboard and an apologetic look.

Opal stares at the clipboard, knowing all of the answers to the medical questions but unable to lift her fingers to grasp the pen. To write down Luca's date of birth, their insurance information or anything else they'd need to know about him, to better care for him. It's almost dizzying to Opal to even try wrapping her mind about what had happened. All he did was slip. He slipped on ice and bumped his head. It couldn't be that bad...could it?

Before Opal can take a chance on wondering the answer to her own question, a doctor approaches her with a bit of a strained look on his face. Causing her heart to jump as she waits to hear what he has to say to her.

"Mrs. Nataro?" The doctor says in a quizzical tone.

"Yes, that's me" Opal confirms as she stands and sets the clipboard down on the chair.

"I'm Doctor Brown, I am on call today and checked out your husband Luca's injuries," Dr. Brown says in a firm tone "Due to his unconsciousness, there is not much I can do. But I am positive he has a concussion, the severity of it is what we have to wait on in order to diagnose how bad it may or may not be."

"So, all we can do is wait for him to wake up?" Opal asks, feeling a lump form in her throat.

"Yes, once he is awake I will be ordering a CT scan to get a look at what's going on inside his head and we will be conducting neurological and cognitive testing" Dr. Brown nods to himself "We will be as thorough as we can so we can give him a correct diagnosis and get him back home with you."

"Okay," Opal nods as well.

"Mrs. Nataro, your husband is in great hands. Why don't you fill out your forms and head home, we can call you once he is awake" Dr. Brown says quietly, his hand gently pats Opal's shoulder.

"That's alright, I'd prefer to sit with him instead," Opal says as she turns and picks up the clipboard.

Dr. Brown nods and moves aside for her to enter Luca's makeshift hospital room. A nurse smiles softly as Opal pulls a chair closer to the edge of Luca's bed. Opal presses a kiss to Luca's forehead before she sits down, tears betraying her and falling down her face anyways. She gives herself a moment to be upset, furiously wiping her face with her sleeve before she forces her attention on the paperwork in front of her.

Opal quickly fills the form out and heads to the nurse's station to give the clipboard back.

"Thank you darling" A woman with bright pink hair smiles at her.

"I was curious, can I stay overnight with my husband? Or can I only be here during visitors' hours? Also, will he be staying in the ER until he wakes up or will he be moved?" Opal inquires, her voice shakier than she'd like.

Opal's fingers tremble as she folds her hands together in an effort to make them stop.

"As his wife, you can stay, you just need a family pass which I can get you. Anyone else can only come during visitors' hours. We will be moving him later tonight to our ICU. There will be a pull-out chair for you to sleep in" The nurse leans closer to Opal and grins devilishly "However, it's wicked uncomfortable. So, you may want to reconsider."

Opal smiles back softly, nodding her head as she tries to swallow despite the dryness in her throat.

"Thank you" Opal manages before she turns and heads back towards Luca's room.

As Opal enters Luca's room this time, she pulls her charger out of her purse and plugs in her phone. Settling into the chair her mind wanders, before she realizes she should call Luca's brother, Stephen.

Luca grew up in a foster home, in California. He never knew his biological parents and formed a close bond with his foster brother, Stephen. Growing up, Luca had attributed a lot of his successes in life to Stephen for pushing him to be better. Stephen was biologically related to Luca's late foster parents and so he and Stephen often got funny looks when they said they were only four months apart.

The trilling makes Opal's head throb, but she keeps her fingers crossed hoping Stephen will answer. Unsurprisingly, he doesn't. Opal leaves a short voicemail anyways and sets her phone back down on the wooden table. She leans on the edge of the mattress, gently caressing Luca's hand in her own as she presses a kiss to his palm.

They'd made it through college together, they made it through harder times than this. Opal could only tell herself that they'd be okay. That the ultimate outcome was them together, Luca was her only endgame.

Chapter Two

Opal wakes up around six in the morning, the awkward position of sleeping in the fold out chair leaves her with a slight headache. Pecking Luca on the cheek before she gathers her purse and leaves, she decides a quick shower in her own bathroom is exactly what she needs. A moment to catch her breath was what the doctor hadn't ordered, but Opal knew she needed, nonetheless.

As Opal steps out of the hospital, puffy white clouds greet her. A soft, but frigid breeze making her shiver as she quickly walks back to their cabin. Their cozy little cabin nestled on the end of a small cul de sac. The white shiplap was what originally sold Opal on the house, too much television about home renovations had ruined her.

Despite the original infatuation with shiplap, Luca had begun to point out more subtle things about the home. Little intricate carvings in the wood of doorways and archways. Little burn marks on the hardwood floors. Even the new windows were placed in the old casing to keep the charming yet modern feel of the cabin, which Opal and Luca felt lucky enough to call home.

As Opal pushes past a loud, whipping rush of wind an older woman comes out of their home with a blanket in her arms. She quickly wraps it around Opal as they hurry inside.

"Thanks, Daria" Opal grins as another shiver escapes her.

"Got to stay warm out there" Daria smiles, her crow's feet becoming more apparent around her upturned shaped eyes "How's the husband?"

"The doctor says he has a concussion but won't know the extent of it until Luca decides to wake up," Opal says as she slowly folds the blanket and sets it down on the sofa.

"Stubborn one he is. I'll keep him in my thoughts." Daria says softly as she gently pats Opal's shoulder.

"Thank you, Daria, for now, I'd just like to shower" Opal murmurs as her hands fly into her pockets.

"Of course, let me get out of your hair. Feel free to let me know if you need anything. I made Nick take that turkey out of that deep fryer before he ruined it. I stuck it in my oven instead" Daria smirks as Opal glances out the window, noticing the giant tub of grease is gone "Whenever Luca is feeling better, we can have a belated Thanksgiving"

"We would love that, thank you," Opal says with a fond look.

Daria simply nods and pats Opal once more on the shoulder before she turns and throws on a heavy parka and heads out of the cabin. Opal watches to make sure she gets home safely, stripping down to nothing once she sees Daria's front door close.

As the warm water falls over Opal, she finds herself anxious to get back to the hospital. To know if Luca is okay and to know once and for all what's going on with his head. Opal washes her long hair, letting memories of them flood her mind at once.

Luca and Opal met during their freshman year of college. She was sitting in a cafe, mulling over which pictures from her latest nature hike to use in her portfolio. One, in particular, had caught Luca's attention as he stood on line. A close-up photo of yellow merrybell flower. He had ordered his coffee and sat down across from her. Initially startling Opal to no end that he took it upon himself to sit down and compliment her work, but she also found something charming about his confidence and the way he wasn't afraid to critique her work while always managing to sound charming.

Opal thinks to the last time they had sat together and looked over her photographs. The moment they landed in Bearsville, Opal had begun snapping photos of everything. Luca watched her adoringly before they stumbled back into the room they were staying in at Ruthie's small B&B. Covered in snow and freezing, Opal let her camera rest before developing the film the next morning. Both her and Luca immediately knowing they'd never want to leave the small town.

Letting out a deep breath of air, Opal finishes rinsing her hair and turns off the water. Cool air hitting her almost immediately when she opens the bathroom door. She walks across the banister lined hallway overlooking the quaint living room as she enters the master bedroom. Quickly blowing drying her hair, applying light makeup and slipping into warm clothes, Opal drives back to the hospital in her and Luca's shared SUV.

As Opal enters the hospital, something in the air feels different. No one seems to notice her as she shows her family pass to the receptionist and makes her way up to the ICU. Each step she takes closer to Luca's room makes her stomach do flips. Makes her heart beat a little faster.

As she rounds the corner, she can hear Dr. Brown's voice and quickens her pace to see who he is speaking to. As Opal steps into the room, she is shocked to see Dr. Brown speaking to an awake and seemingly alert Luca.

Luca looks at Opal and her heart skips a beat, instantly realizing that he doesn't recognize her. He doesn't look at her as the love of his life, the look in his eyes is distant.... empty.

Luca looks at Opal as though she is a stranger, someone he didn't share breathtaking memories with. Opal immediately wonders what will happen if he doesn't remember their relationship, their love or their life together.

"You're awake..." Opal stutters as she further enters the room, standing at the foot of Luca's bed.

Before Luca can respond, Dr. Brown ushers Opal out of the room, closing the door behind him. The look on his face confirms Opal's worst nightmares, though she tries not to let it bother her.

"Luca has suffered a rather severe head injury. We are still figuring out just how severe, but he believes that it is the year two thousand and eleven" Dr. Brown looks over his notes "He seems to be unable to recall the last seven years, believing instead that he has just graduated high school"

Opal takes a step back, her heart nearly on the cold tile of the hospital floor as panic floods her system. Luca can't remember the last seven years. Luca and Opal met during the late fall of two thousand and eleven. Maybe if she could trigger a memory from then, maybe he'd remember everything.

"Opal?" Dr. Brown asks as he gently touches her forearm.

"Sorry, sorry" Opal shakes her head, trying to blink back the tears that form against her will in her eyes "What do we do now?"

"I know it's hard, but we have to give him time. Maybe go home while we run some tests and bring back some mementos from your time together. Nothing too intimate, but things that only the two of you shared together." Dr. Brown nods "Perhaps a game you both love or something from a hobby the two of you share."

Opal nods, her mind racing a million miles a minute as she instantly compiles a list of things to bring back with her.

"I have a top neurologist flying in and our on-call psychologist will arrive any minute. I can promise you that he will be okay." Dr. Brown pauses briefly "However, please consider that he may not be the same. His emotions and reactions to his environment may be changed."

All Opal can muster is a slow nod and a small smile. She looks through the glass panel on Luca's door one more time before she leaves. Her tears betraying her as she climbs back into the SUV.

Chapter Three

Minutes go by, Opal trying to regain her composure but every second only heightens her emotions more. Tears flow down her face like water rushes down the Niagara. Her heart aches more than it ever has before. Opal feels almost as though Luca had left her, packed his bags and departed.

After slamming her fist into the steering wheel, Opal finally manages to calm down. Starting the car and turning the heat all the way up as she drives back home, her fingers crossed that for once, Daria won't be there to ask how Luca is.

As though her thoughts are read by a higher power, Daria is nowhere in sight as Opal pulls the SUV into the garage and quickly hurries inside. Kicking off her snow boots by the door, she quickly gets to work on finding items that may help Luca remember their relationship. First things first, her portfolio. The first thing he noticed about her, was her photography. More specifically, the merrybells. Opal dashes up the wooden staircase and past the master bedroom to a door at the very end of the hall. The only other door on that level of the house. It creaks as she pushes it open to reveal an even creakier staircase. The attic remains a place Opal does not like, but she pushes her distaste aside to quickly find her college portfolio.

Once she's opened at least half a dozen dusty boxes, she finds the portfolio. Blowing off a thick layer of dust and sneezing from her choice of action in cleaning the portfolio, she closes the boxes back up. Opal quickly makes her way back downstairs and gives her old portfolio a thorough cleaning. She grabs a reusable bag from the cabinet under the microwave and tosses in the portfolio. On top of that goes a copy of Luca's college diploma, a small bottle of sand from a vacation in Madrid as well as a silver earring, from when Luca thought it'd be cool to pierce his septum.

Without wanting to bring too many things, Opal also tosses in a photo album of pictures they'd taken together during their travels and heads back to the hospital. As she pulls into the parking lot, she curses under her breath at how slow time had gone by. She felt so eager and the mother time was willing to torture her.

Opal tries everything to make the time go faster. Playing her favorite songs through the car's speaker, channeling her inner Spice Girl before trying to take a nap. She even goes down to the hospital's cafe for a cup of coffee, only to discover she's burnt a total of ten minutes. Giving up on trying to avoid seeing Luca, Opal tosses her to go cup in the garbage and heads up to the ICU. Noticing a couple more medical professionals in his room, Opal sits on a chair in the hallway. Her back to the large, glass windows as her toes tap impatiently against the cool tile.

Waiting...waiting...waiting...

Dr. Brown and his new team emerge from Luca's room. Dr. Brown chuckles as he takes in Opal's demeanor.

"After some evaluation, I have decided to diagnose Luca with a Traumatic Brain Injury, or TBI for short" Dr. Brown says calmly as Opal nods along "He has some head pain, memory loss and is rather emotional and confused."

"I brought somethings that may help him remember, has he made any progress on remembering?" Opal asks a bit too eagerly as she scoots forward in her seat.

"One thing at a time, right now we are watching his brain for swelling. Once he is out of the clear with that, we will work on getting his memory back. You are welcome to try, however, don't push him or get mad if he insists, he doesn't remember" Dr. Brown lets out a small breath of air, almost as though he had been holding it "Also, try to keep your emotions in check. I can only imagine how it must feel for your spouse to not remember your relationship, but he is unwell at the moment. This won't last forever"

"Of course, I just want to be with him right now. Make sure he's okay." Opal says as her lower lips trembles a bit.

Dr. Brown nods and motions for Opal to go ahead and enter Luca's room. She gives Dr. Brown a warm smile and slowly enters Luca's room, not wanting to startle him.

"Hey, you," Opal says softly as she closes the door behind her "How are you feeling?"

Luca watches Opal for a moment, his lips in a straight line as he ponders her. Wondering if he knows her or if she works for the hospital. His head slightly throbbing.

"I am alright," Luca says as his fingers gently rub his temples "I've got a killer headache though…"

"I bet, did they tell you what happened?" Opal asks as she pulls a wooden-legged chair closer to Luca's bed.

Luca simply shakes his head, words seemingly lost from his lips as Opal smiles softly at him.

"You fell on a walkway. Slipped on some ice and bumped your head" Opal says so softly it feels as though she is whispering.

She wasn't sure if she should be so honest with him. Though Dr. Brown's advice was clear to anyone listening, Opal still wondered just how much detail she should tell Luca about.

"A walkway?" Luca questions, causing Opal to shift uncomfortably in her seat.

"Yes…outside of our home," Opal says quickly, afraid that if she had not then she wouldn't have said it at all.

Luca's eyes flit from the white wall across from his bed to Opal. His demeanor changing from that of confusion to simply perplexed at Opal's statement.

"Our…" Luca whispers the word.

"Yes, our," Opal replies boldly, holding up her left ring finger.

Luca's eyes widen as he stares at Opal's rather large ring. It wasn't your typical diamond wedding band combo. Instead, Luca had put Opal's birthstone, aquamarine, on a ring and gave it to her as a gift, which she had mistaken for an engagement ring. When they ran off and eloped, they purchased a set of wooden wedding bands. However, when those became impractical, they ventured into a flea market outside of Wales to find silicone wedding rings with waves from the ocean carefully painted all around the outside.

Most days, Opal opted to wear just her wedding band, finding it more comfortable than a metal band anyways.

Luca visibly gulps and looks down to his ring finger, to find the same blue silicone band resting on his finger. After a moment, he looks back at Opal with a sense of humility in his eyes.

"Did Stephen send you to prank me?" Luca snorts as he rolls his eyes.

"No, this isn't a prank," Opal says as she feels herself blushing.

"I mean, you're gorgeous. I would probably marry you once I got to know you, but there is no way. I'm about to be nineteen..." Luca trails off, but Opal is no longer listening.

Opal sets down the reusable bag on the end of Luca's bed and steps out into the hallway as he continues to babble to himself. Luca was back to his old self. The young, rowdy, irrational boy that Opal fell in love with despite his shortcomings. After the last seven years, Luca had become more well-rounded and smarter, he became more aware of not just his own feelings but Opal's as well. Thinking that their wedding bands were a prank was definitely twenty eleven Luca.

Chapter Four

Opal wasn't sure how long she'd been standing out in the cold air for. The skin on her hands felt frigid, so frigid in fact that when her phone rang, she partially worried she'd break off part of her finger answering the call.

"Hello?" Opal says into her phone as she turns and walks back into the hospital.

"Hey, I got your voicemail. What happened to Luca?" A man says into the line, Opal instantly recognizes as Luca's foster brother, Stephen.

"He fell yesterday and hit his head. The doctor says he has a Mild Brain injury and since he woke up, he believes that it is 2011 and he has just graduated high school" Opal says into the phone as her fingers regain feeling.

"Shit," Stephen says as Opal imagines him pacing around the boardwalk where he lives in California "I'll fly out as soon as I can get a flight"

"Thank you, I'll keep you updated. We are still in the hospital, I'm not sure when he will be discharged." Opal says slowly.

"Alright," Stephen replies "And Opal?"

"Yeah?"

"Try not to worry"

"No Promises"

Opal ends the call and slips her phone back into her pocket. She breathes slowly into her palms, as her hands folded over her mouth. The relief coming instantly as feeling returns to her hands. Opal makes her way back up to Luca's room, wondering if he's flushed his wedding band down the toilet yet.

"Hey wife" Luca teases as Opal enters the room again.

"Hey, husband" Opal teases back despite how much Luca's word sting.

"So, if we are married, where did we get married?" Luca questions as he arches an eyebrow at her.

"In Wales, near a small town by where my mother grew up" Opal responds back as she takes a seat on the side of Luca's bed.

"And why would we get married there? That sounds hella weird" Luca says nonchalantly, despite his eyebrows momentarily crinkling.

Opal sits silently for a moment, trying to remind herself that this is the old Luca. The immature Luca. The Luca she never would have married had he not matured sometime during their sophomore year of college.

"I wanted us to be married near some family. Stephen flew out with us; my mom and brother came as well." Opal drops her voice down to barely a whisper "It was extremely beautiful and touching"

Luca seems to catch on to the one emotion Opal is actually allowing herself to convey, passion. He watches her almost intensely as she takes a deep breath. Reminding herself repeatedly that he would remember the happiest day of their lives together again, he just would.

"Sorry if I hurt your feelings, this is just...weird," Luca says firmly.

"I understand, I think I should head back home. Let you rest and focus on getting your memories back." Opal says as dismay flashes across her face.

"I'll...see you at home then," Luca says encouragingly, if not too playful for Opal's liking.

Without thinking, Opal stands and leans down to kiss Luca. Red flooding her face when she realizes she was about to kiss him. Embarrassment filling her to her core as she pecks Luca lightly on the cheek and straightens back up. Neither says a word as Opal gathers her purse, her hand reaching for the reusable bag before she decides to leave it. Maybe looking through it alone would jog his memory.

At least she hoped it would.

As Opal leaves, she texts Stephen an update who confirms he's found a flight out for three days from then. Opal breathes a sigh of relief, hoping that Stephen will be able to do some good. Opal pulls off her family visiting pass and stuffs it deep into her purse, breathing in a deep breath of icy mountain air. As Opal pulls into her driveway, she spots Nick and Adeleine on her front porch. Opal had no issue with Adeleine at the moment, but she was worried about what she would be saying to Nick in a moment.

Opal shuts off the car and tries to bury her anger as she gets out of the car. Shutting the door harder than she means to as she walks up onto the porch.

"Opal..." Adeleine says softly as she pulls Opal into a tight hug "I am so so sorry"

Opal doesn't respond, simply hugging Adeleine back as she glares at Nick. Nick tries at all costs to avoid Opal's gaze until Adeleine forces him up onto his feet and nudges him towards Adeleine. He approaches her like a dog with its tail between its legs. Fully aware that its owner is not happy due to some rotten doggy behavior.

"Sorry about Lucs..." Nick says as his gaze flits everywhere except to Opal "If it makes you feel better, we didn't even get to fry the turkey. Your neighbor came over and stole it, sent us all home hungry."

"Good," Opal says through gritted teeth "Your moronic idea to fry a beautiful bird carcass is the whole reason Luca is in this mess."

Nick stares blankly at Opal, enraging her even more than she had been, to begin with. Everyone knew that Nick wasn't the brightest bulb in the bunch but the fact that he couldn't sincerely apologize about Luca made Opal   feel   worse.

"Is that all you want to say?" Opal says as her lips form in a thin, straight line.

Nick nods and moves off of the porch like a child who has just been scolded. Adeleine rubs her temples as she approaches Opal once again.

"I really am sorry for both of us," Adeleine says as tears form in her eyes.

Opal nods and moves aside for Adeleine to leave with Nick. She watches Adeleine pull him back towards the car, both of them getting in and driving off as Adeleine wipes her eyes. Opal lets out the breath she didn't realize she had been holding and heads back inside. Intending to spend the next couple of days trying to focus on herself, at least until Stephen's plane lands

Chapter Five

Opal rolls over in bed, the sheets next to her still fairly in place and cool. Tears sting her eyes as she quickly blinks them back, willing herself not to lose it. The last three days have gone by in a haze. Opal cleaning things that weren't dirty, to begin with, as well as trying to get into photographer mode with some new photos to hang around the cabin.

She's barely sitting up in bed when a knock on the door pulls her from her thoughts. The clock reads a quarter to eight in the morning and Opal knew exactly who'd be standing on her doorstep. She throws on a pair of sweats and a hoodie and quickly makes her way downstairs, swinging open the oak door to reveal Stephen, Luca's brother, on the front porch.

"Good Morning Beautiful" Stephen grins as Opal steps outside to hug him.

"Normally I'd roll my eyes, but you have no idea how good it is to see you right now," Opal says as a slight shiver runs down her spine.

Stephen laughs as he picks up his suitcase and follows Opal back inside. Already having stayed with them before, Stephen walks right into the guest bedroom and sets his suitcase down while Opal puts on a pot of coffee and heats up some pastries.

"Are you hungry? Or hangry?" Opal calls out to Stephen.

"Girl you know I'm always hangry!" Stephen calls back to her.

Opal chuckles as she pulls a large bowl of mixed fruit out of the refrigerator. An array of pastries and fruit rest on the eat-in kitchens table, Stephen taking a seat as soon as the coffee is finished. Opal brings over two mugs and the steaming pot of coffee while Stephen hops up and grabs milk and creamer from the refrigerator.

They both settle back down at the table, Opal resting the pot of coffee on a warmer as she slices the top off of a blueberry muffin and puts butter both sides. Stephen pours a bit of heavy cream into his coffee as a sigh of relief spreads across his lips.

"So, run me through what happened again?" Stephen asks as he sets down his mug.

"Our friend Nick had an idea to deep fry our turkey outside, for whatever reason Luca agreed. Well they were about to deep fry the turkey when Luca runs over to me on the porch to confirm that I have the camera when he slips and bangs his head against the ground" Opal shudders at the memory "We got him to the hospital and he woke up the next morning where the doctor confirmed he has a TBI…"

"And what's the part about him thinking he just graduated high school?" Stephen asks, keeping his gaze on Opal.

"He suffered some memory loss from the fall, he thinks he is in two thousand and eleven. He thinks he is about to go off to college. He doesn't recognize me at all" Opal sighs.

Stephen dramatically wipes his eyes and stands to pull Opal into a tight hug. He holds her close to him, his hand gently patting the back of her head before they both sit back down.

"Have you seen him since the diagnosis?" Stephen asks.

Opal chews on her lower lip, wishing she had gone but knowing it'd just hurt her more. Opal knows Stephen won't judge her for going back, they'd formed a solid friendship since Opal and Luca started getting serious, but not going back to the hospital really did weight heavily on her. No matter how many mini wreaths she made in hopes to make the gnawing feeling go away.

"I haven't. It's too hard" Opal shakes her head slowly as she says the words she hadn't wanted to.

"I get it. I do. Do you know when he will be discharged? Is he coming back here?" Stephen asks.

"I'd like for him to come back here, but I am not going to force him," Opal says quietly.

Stephen nods and finishes off the last of his coffee. His lips parted slightly as a look of defeat splashes across his face.

"I'll go see him now, get a feel for how he's doing. When he gets discharged do you want to pick him up?" Stephen asks as he watches Opal carefully.

"Sure" Opal simply nods nonchalantly.

"Are you sure you don't want to come with me? I think it could be good, maybe he's made some progress." Stephen says encouragingly, a smile on his lips once again.

Opal meets his gaze, her heart pounding out of her chest, wanting nothing more than to go with Stephen to see Luca. But at the same time, her heart aches at the thought of him being unable to remember her again.

"Opal...no one can forget someone as amazing as you," Stephen says softly as he nods towards the front door.

Opal gives in, not only to Stephen but also to the tears she denied earlier in the morning. Stephen helps Opal clean up and flips through their Netflix while Opal gets changed. They both get into the SUV, Stephen shivering relentlessly.

"I don't know how you two do it, I left sunny and eighty-degree weather for snow and negative four degrees" Stephen shudders as he looks at the snow falling outside of his window.

"Technically it's negative seven" Opal laughs as her finger taps the car's thermometer.

Stephen curses under his breath as they wait for the heat to kick in and warm them up. Sadly, for him, by the time Opal pulls into the hospital's parking lot, the car is semi-warm.

Stephen and Opal get out of the SUV, quickly heading inside to get visitors passes before heading up to see Luca. When they arrive in his room, he's asleep. His hair a mess on his head Opal hangs back, letting Stephen take center stage.

Stephen licks his finger and sticks it in Luca's earlobe, much to Opal's disgust. Luca jerks awake, an alarmed look on his face before he realizes who stuck their wet finger in his ear.

"Bro!" Luca grins at Stephen as they quickly one arm hug.

"Look who I brought with me" Stephen grins at Luca.

Luca turns and looks right at Opal, her heart skipping a beat as her palms get sweatier. Her mind consumed with thoughts about Luca and if he'd remember her this time.

"Opal..." Luca says softly "Girl from the coffee shop"

Chapter Six

The ache in Opal's heart slowly lessens as Luca slowly begins to remember more and more of the last seven years. So far, he seems to be remembering the first semester of their freshman years. They met at the end of September and by Halloween, he had managed to weasel his way into her heart. The rest was seemingly history. History that Opal felt she'd need to rehash like word vomit in the upcoming days, weeks or even months.

"Opal?" Stephen says, breaking Opal out of her thoughts.

"Sorry, what's up?" Opal asks as she looks towards where Stephen sits next to Luca's empty bed.

"Luca is changing his clothes, so he can be discharged, you ready to take him home?" Stephen asks.

"Beyond ready, home hasn't been the same without him," Opal says softly as she stands from her chair "I'll go get the car started."

Stephen nods as Opal leaves the room, heading down to the parking garage and getting the SUV nice and warm for Luca. A few minutes later, Luca and Stephen emerge from the exit and get into the car with Opal. The snow lightening up from when Opal and Stephen first arrived earlier in the day. Luca buckles his seat belt, glancing over at Opal in the driver seat as she takes off.

The drive back to the cottage is quick, most of their neighbors waiting outside in the cold to see Luca. Daria smiles as soon as she sees the SUV pull up, but from the thin line of Opal's lips, Daria waves everyone away. Allowing Opal to pull into the garage without any interference.

"So, we live here?" Luca asks as she slowly unbuckles himself.

"Yep" Opal replies "We bought it almost a year ago"

Luca nods, closing the car door and waiting for Opal to show him the door to get inside. Opal pushes open a regular sized oak door and Luca enters their home, his eyes going over everything. The open concept with the living room flowing neatly into the kitchen with a large, round dining table off to the side. Near the front door is a reading nook, next to that a bedroom before a couple more doors and a staircase leading up to an open hallway with railways on both sides until double doors appear on one end and a singular oak door on the other.

"Did you decorate?" Luca asks, motioning to a large wreath over the small fireplace.

"Yes, I made that after we moved in, this Christmas will be our first in this house," Opal says softly.

Everyone shrugs off their jackets, Stephen slinking away to the kitchen to make himself a Keurig pod of coffee while Luca sits down awkwardly on the couch.

"So where will I sleep?" Luca asks Opal "I get we're married or whatever, but it feels like I just met you a couple of days ago and sleeping in the same bed may be..."

"Weird" Opal finishes his sentence as she walks around the couch and sits down in an armchair.

Luca nods in her direction, his eyes still going over all of the decorations, the homey and inviting feel of the cabin.

"Stephen is in the guest bedroom, but the bed is a trundle, so you could pull out the bottom mattress and the two of you could work that situation out" Opal grins slightly at Luca.

"Just like when we were kids" Luca chuckles as he looks back at Stephen, who isn't listening to them.

"If you want, I can show you where your closet is. You could bring some things down here to have on hand..." Opal says quietly, feeling like a giant rock is sitting in the pit of her stomach.

"I guess it'd be easier to just keep some clothes down here," Luca says as they both stand.

Opal walks up the steps first, Luca following her as they both make their way into the master bedroom. The large windows overlooking the mountainside makes Luca stop in the doorway. He blinks a couple times, his light green eyes adjusting to the splendor that is the mountainsides of Bearsville. How bright the snow is, how it covers nearly everything in sight. Large pines cover both sides of trails and pathways up the mountain as skiers smile on their way down the other side.

"I would be lying if I said this was the only reason, we bought this house" Opal chuckles, pushing the curtains further open.

"The view is amazing..." Luca says in awe, his jaw slack.

Opal grins, giving him a moment to take in the view.

"There was something in the basement..." Luca says, turning to face Opal "Not a dead body I hope"

Opal arches an eyebrow at Luca, a coy smile on her lips as she walks towards the double doors leading to the hallway.

"Well, only one way to find out..." Opal laughs softly as she walks down the hall.

Luca throws one last glance out of the large window and follows Opal, both of them making their way past Stephen on the phone in the kitchen and to another door right off of the mudroom. Luca pulls the door open and his arm instantly lifts to turn on the light above the stairs.

"Muscle memory is a crazy thing," Opal says softly as they make their way down into the basement.

The basement is probably warmer than the main floor of the house. The downside with all of the large windows was that not all of them were one hundred percent insulated and cold air somehow always found a way in. In the basement, the furnace quietly rumbles in the background as their feet go from dark hardwood floors to plush carpet.

The previous owner had been nice enough to fix up the basement, giving Opal and Luca more livable space. Luca walks past the living room and the bar and swings open a French door right before a half set of stairs.

Opal follows him and watches as a slight smile forms on his lips as they enter the wine cellar. The rectangular room hosts a full wall of wine bottles. Most labeled and others not. Bottles of wine from all over the world, even some from the local Italian restaurant, one of three restaurants you could find in Bearsville. At the end of the room is a small square built in filled with wine glasses, several drawers next to the display.

"As soon as my head injury is resolved, we'll have to revisit" Luca chuckles "I'd enjoy getting to know you again over a Petite Sirah"

Opal blushes softly as she turns away from Luca, her fingers lingering over the exact bottle he is thinking of. Luca takes a second look over the room before looking at Opal. He walks closer to her, his fingers tracing over hers atop of the same bottle of wine.

"You found it..." Luca says softly as he lets his fingers rest on Opal's.

"I know all of your favorites" Opal whispers, her eyes still averted from his.

Luca nods, moving his fingers away from hers as he clears his throat. Opal follows him out of the wine cellar, Luca making his way back up to the master bedroom to collect some of his clothing, while Opal pulls a bottle of white wine from the wine cooler in the kitchen. Pouring herself a healthy serving as Stephen arches his eyebrow at her.

"Shut up" Opal manages in between sips.

Stephen let's out a low laugh, eventually turning his attention back to his phone.

Chapter Seven

Luca finds himself awake earlier than he'd like to be. His thoughts all over the place, unable to be reigned in to sort through. To make sense of. Luca felt a growing frustration in the pit of his stomach. Opal would do or say things and he'd think about her saying it in a different place and outfit. He had to remind himself all of the time that these were memories.

Opal in the red dress, the same red dress she wore on their first date. She made him pancakes and burned the edges like she has done every single time she's made him pancakes. Luca rolls over on the bottom mattress of the trundle bed, his back to Stephen who snores softly behind him. It'd been almost a week and Stephen was due to fly back to California soon. His job needed him and while Luca understood, he also worried he'd feel even more lonely without him there to be a buffer whenever Luca felt lost for words.

He knew deep down that he would be okay, he just wasn't sure how. Knowing he wasn't going to get back to sleep anytime soon, Luca gets up slowly and leaves the guest bedroom. Part of him felt like a stranger in his own house and part of him still couldn't believe he'd come from a poor neighborhood in California to this.

This beautiful life with a beautiful woman and he couldn't even remember it.

Luca notices a soft glow from the kitchen, Opal sits just outside on the porch swing. The tip of her thick slippers slowly pushing the swing back and forth, a steaming mug in her hands. Her long dark hair rests in a braid behind her back, Luca struck by how stunning she is in pajamas and a thick robe. He follows the smell of the dark roast, pouring himself a mug with cinnamon creamer before stepping out onto the porch with Opal.

"Couldn't sleep either?" Luca grins as he stands in front of her.

"Nope. Want to join me?" Opal asks, patting the spot next to her for him to sit.

Luca nods and sits down next to her, both of them rocking the swing slowly as the sun is barely visible in the sky. The snow alone lighting up the dark early morning around them.

"I was thinking about your dress," Luca says quietly.

Opal looks at him, confusion splashed across her face as she waits for him to explain.

"I just mean, the red dress you wore to dinner the other night. I remember you wearing it on our first date" Luca laughs softly before resuming sipping on his coffee.

"You took me to Joe's" Opal grins, the memory replaying in her mind "That little pizza place where the pizza wasn't even edible, everyone went there for the cannoli"

"And of course, the night we went, they had none because we got there so late" Luca smirks in Opal's direction "So we settled for a slice of greasy pizza."

"I had gotten so sick the next morning" Opal shakes her head slowly "I knew better but was having such a good time with you..."

Luca smiles as his eyes flit to the ground. The memory playing in his mind so clearly, he feels as though if he were to close his eyes he'd be transported back in time. A cool breeze sends a chill down Luca's spine, Opal unfolds a blanket that had been sitting on the table next to her and places it over both of them.

"You're insane for coming out here in a t-shirt" Opal grins at Luca.

Luca doesn't say anything back, instead grinning back at Opal. Scooting closer to her as their knees gently touch. Luca knew he was attracted to Opal the moment he saw her in the window of the coffee shop. It wasn't love at first sight, but Luca knew that for the first time in his life, he felt the *need* to know Opal.

While Luca is lost in his head, Opal sets down her mug and leans in closer to Luca. Without even realizing it, Luca gently wraps his arm around Opal's shoulders, the feeling normal. Comfortable. They settle into the porch swing, Opal wanting nothing more than to tilt her face towards Luca and kiss him, but she also is enjoying the moment too much to try ruining it by moving it fast.

"I really should try to get some sleep," Opal says softly "I have an appointment later this morning"

"An appointment?" Luca asks as they gently rock back and forth.

"Yep, just a checkup," Opal whispers, letting out a soft yawn.

"Then let's get you back to bed" Luca whispers back.

They both stand, Opal folding the blanket back up and Luca carrying their mugs back into the kitchen. He turns off the coffee pot warmer, as Opal folds the blanket and places it back on the couch. Opal turns and watches as Luca rinses out the mugs before he walks around the island, both of them awkwardly standing in front of each other.

"I don't want to push..." Opal sighs, her finger kneading into her robe "Do you think you could sleep with me...in our bedroom? Just this once?"

Luca nods, feeling his heart beat out of his chest as he follows Opal upstairs. They both climb into bed, Opal resting her head against Luca's chest, knowing she wouldn't wake up in this position but at the moment it was what she needed.

"Goodnight" Opal whispers as her eyelids become heavier and heavier.

"Or Good Morning" Luca whispers back as he tilts his head to look out the large window.

Opal let's out a barely audible laugh as Luca makes himself comfortable. Both of them snuggled up together, the sun barely in the sky as they fall back to sleep.

"Hey, Opal..." Luca says softly, his finger gently brushing against Opal's cheek.

"Hm..." Opal grumbles, her face tilted up towards his despite her eyes still closed.

"Do you mind if I just stay up here? The pull-out trundle bed is...uncomfortable" Luca asks.

"I've missed you" Opal whispers in response.

Luca grins, tugging her closer to him as they slowly fall back asleep.

Chapter Eight

The smell of burning food jolts both Opal and Luca up and out of bed. Opal slips her feet into her slippers while Luca heads downstairs. Opal walks downstairs to see Luca throwing a cast iron pan outside into the snow, while Stephen holds the sink sprayer towards the stovetop, water splashing everywhere.

Opal stands at the bottom of the staircase, her jaw practically on the floor as she watches Luca come back inside and shut off the water to the sink. Stephen turns to face them both slowly, an apologetic look spread across his face as he slowly sets down the sink sprayer next to the faucet.

"I figured I'd make breakfast..." Stephen shrugs, his cheeks tinting pink "I was hungry, and I wasn't sure what you two were doing upstairs."

"We were sleeping, really?" Luca shakes his head as he turns towards Opal.

"I mean...we have cereal..." Opal says, the shock slowly wearing off as she walks towards the kitchen.

Luca comes back out of the mudroom with a mop in one hand and towels cut up for rags in the other. He and Opal get to cleaning up the wet kitchen while Stephen steps out, hoping that bagels will make up for his mess.

Once Luca and Opal finish mopping up all of the water, Opal takes the mop and rags back to the mudroom. Tossing the rags into the washer and putting the mop away, Opal enters the kitchen again to find Luca making more coffee.

"I don't know how we cleaned before coffee..." Opal grins as she grabs mugs from the cabinet.

"Me neither" Luca laughs as he waits for the coffee to finish brewing.

Opal pulls herself up onto the counter, her feet dangling in front of her as a silence falls between them. Luca turns around, bumping into Opal's knees as they meet each other's gaze. A smile forms on both of their lips, Luca's hands sliding slowly up Opal's thighs. Opal shifts, allowing Luca to step closer to her as the coffee pot dings that the coffee is ready.

"Ignore it..." Opal whispers.

"That was the plan" Luca whispers back, his eyes on her lips.

Luca leans forward, Opal impatiently grabbing the collar of his shirt, causing their lips to collide. Luca's hands drop onto the counter, his palms pressed into the cold marble as Opal loops her arms around Luca's neck.

Both of them melting into the kiss. After a moment, Opal pulls back, nearly lying flat against the counter as Luca steps back for her to sit up.

"So" Opal grins "How much do you remember now?"

Luca let's out a low laugh, planting another kiss on her cheek this time before he steps back slightly to look at her.

"To be honest, I've been feeling like I remember everything, just out of order," Luca says as his fingers slide to the edge of the counter "For example, we graduated and moved into that tiny studio apartment? Or we moved in before we graduated?"

"We moved into a studio apartment while we were still in college and after graduation upgraded to a one bedroom" Opal chuckles "Neither had a tub so still unsure if it really was an upgrade."

Luca looks away for a moment before he looks back at Opal, a more serious expression on his face.

"I can remember our wedding, with your mom and brother and Stephen..." Luca trails off before clearing his throat "I can't seem to remember proposing to you, however"

A soft smile settles on Opal's lips as she leans forward slightly. Her voice low,

"You didn't propose"

Luca looks even more confused than before. He takes a step back, wondering what happened that they decided to jump ship and get married without him proposing.

"I'm confused," Luca says as he leans against the opposite counter.

46

"After graduation, we flew out to see my mom and brother in Wales. While we were there, we just decided to get married, we found our wedding bands shortly after in a flea market. It all came together quite nicely" Opal says thinking back on the memory "Even Stephen flew out"

"Stephen did what now?" Stephen laughs as he walks back into the cabin.

"I was telling Luca that you flew out for our wedding," Opal says over her shoulder.

Stephen shakes off his coat as he sets down a brown bag and a tray of to go mugs on the counter. Before removing his coat and hanging it up.

"It was beautiful, please tell me you remember marrying this gorgeous specimen of a woman" Stephen grins as he pulls Opal off of the counter and spins her around.

Luca stays pressed against the opposite counter before he storms upstairs. Opal looks at Stephen, both of them confused. Opal begins to walk up the steps when Luca comes bounding down the steps and storms out of the house. Stephen grabs his coat and runs after him, leaving Opal standing at the bottom of the staircase completely bewildered.

Opal checks the time, quickly grabbing a muffin out of the brown bag that Stephen brought by before she heads upstairs and gets dressed for her appointment.

-

Luca runs down a side street in the small town of Bearsville, stopping momentarily in front of a foot of snow leading into a thick forest of trees until he hears Stephen running up behind him. Frustrated, he steps into the snow and walks quickly into the thick forest, disappearing into the pines.

"Luca come on!" Stephen calls out as he follows Luca's footprints in the dense snow.

Luca finds a low hanging tree branch and jumps up onto it. Snow shaking off the branch and colliding with the ground as he sits on the thick branch, waiting for Stephen to catch up with him. Stephen stops short in front of Luca on the branch, his chest quickly heaving as he glares at Luca.

"Are you kidding me?" Stephen asks through ragged breathing.

"I never proposed to her..." Luca says quietly, feeling the heat rise in his cheeks "How could she marry me?"

"I don't understand why you're so hung up on details, she married you in the end" Stephen huffs as clouds of his breath form in front of his face "Why are you so mad you didn't propose?"

Luca runs his hand across his forehead, gently rubbing his temples before looking at Stephen again.

"When I met Opal, she was sitting in this little cafe going over her portfolio. She had wrinkles all over her forehead because she was so concerned about getting it right" Luca grins "That's who she is. She wants to do things the right way, she changed her beliefs for me. In Wales, I should have proposed. Not go along with the plan for some shotgun wedding"

Stephen takes another moment to catch his breath, a smirk on his lips as Luca balls up snow and tosses it at him.

"Listen, if you want to propose to her, then do it" Stephen laughs as he ducks under a snowball.

"We are already married..." Luca says in a mocking tone.

Stephen rolls his eyes as he balls up some snow, hurling it at Luca's head before he speaks again.

"What does it matter? Old people renew their vows, why can't you propose to your wife? Especially when you ran out on her like that, not cool" Stephen grins as Luca hops down from the tree branch.

"Alright, I think I will then" Luca grins "Want to help me pick out a ring?"

Stephen checks his watch before he nods at Luca.

"Sure, then you got to take me to the airport" Stephen chuckles.

"Deal"

Stephen tosses his arm around Luca's neck, tousling his hair as they walk back towards the small town and out of the thick pine forest.

Chapter Nine

Opal arrives back from her appointment, feeling a wide array of emotions. From excitement to nervousness to scared. When she gets back, Stephen's suitcase sits on the front porch, him and Luca sitting in the living room.

"Hey," Opal says softly as she enters the house.

"Hey Opal," Stephen says as he stands up "Luca is going to drive me to the airport, want to come with us?"

"No, it's okay, I think I'm going to have lunch with Adeleine," Opal says Stephen pulls her into a hug "Have a safe flight"

"Sun is out, and snow looks like it's melting, have fun at lunch" Stephen chuckles.

"Snow here never melts" Opal laughs as Luca nods.

Luca slips his jacket on as him and Stephen leave, climbing into the SUV with his suitcase as Opal stands on the porch and waves them goodbye. Almost as if on cue, Adeleine pulls up in front of the house, Opal locking the front door behind her as she hops down the steps carefully and gets into Adeleine's car.

"Hey, you" Opal grins "Where are we headed for lunch?"

"I thought we could take a little drive, head over to Lake Pine" Adeleine replies.

"What on earth is in Lake Pine?" Opal asks as she cocks her head sideways at Adeleine.

"Nick got a job as a sous chef at a cute little bistro which serves French food" Adeleine chuckles.

"Are you kidding me? The man wanted to deep fry my precious Turkey and now he is a sous chef?" Opal asks as she arches her eyebrows at Adeleine.

Adeleine shrugs as she pulls onto a road that links Bearsville and Lake Pine. Opal decides to relax and enjoy the view, despite how irritated she still was with Nick.

About twenty minutes later, Adeleine pulls into the parking lot with a small, off-white building as the focus. Adeleine parks relatively close to the building and they step out, the smell of pine and burning wood fill the town.

"You know, I'm glad Bearsville doesn't live up to its name" Opal chuckles as she links arms with Adeleine.

"Me too, can you imagine? The deer are nosey enough" Adeleine laughs as they enter the building.

A hostess smiles at them, walking them over to a small table near a large window. A moment later a waitress comes over before they've even had a chance to take their coats off. They place their drinks orders while she gives them a minute to mule over the menu.

The waitress comes back and sets their drinks on the table. Before leaving she takes their order and retrieves the menus. Adeleine and Opal zone in on their drinks before Opal grins at Adeleine.

"What?" Adeleine asks as she sets down her mug.

"I had a doctor's appointment this morning and I was kind of taken aback by the diagnosis," Opal says quietly as Adeleine leans forward in her chair.

"Is it bad?" Adeleine asks.

"Well I'm not sure yet, we'll know in about nine months," Opal says as she breaks out into a wide smile.

"You're pregnant?!" Adeleine shouts, her hands flying over her mouth as she looks apologetically around the restaurant.

"Yes," Opal laughs "With everything going on I didn't even realize. The last few weeks have flown by"

"I mean, it makes sense. You were kind of cranky on Thanksgiving." Adeleine smirks.

"Well yeah, your knuckle brained husband wanted to fry my turkey," Opal says as the smile fades from her lips momentarily.

Adeleine reaches across the small table to take Opal's hands in her own. A soft smile on her lips as a sincere expression fills her face.

"He really is sorry, he just doesn't know how to say it" Adeleine grins "You have bigger things coming your way anyways, how's Luca doing? Have you told him yet?"

"He's good. He remembers almost everything he just seems to have trouble piecing it together in order sometimes" Opal says softly "And no, I haven't told him yet. I haven't wanted to scare him"

"How could you possibly scare him? The man is hopelessly in love with you" Adeleine chuckles as the waitress comes back with their food.

"Thank you" Opal smiles at the waitress "The timing isn't right"

Adeleine moves her hands from Opal's as she keeps her gaze on Opal. Adeleine waits for the waitress to leave before she resumes talking.

"The timing probably won't ever be, but you can bite the bullet or hand him a baby one day," Adeleine says as she zones in on her food.

"I suppose..." Opal smirks at Adeleine "You have a point"

"See? I told you I'm always right. Why do you think Nick married me? I'm a genius" Adeleine giggles.

"I love Nick, but a tree is intelligent next to him," Opal says laughing softly.

Both Adeleine and Opal focus on the food in front of them, the conversation dying down to a comfortable silence before Adeleine excuses herself to go see Nick. Opal watches as they step outside.

Nobody knew what brought Nick and Adeleine together. They were seemingly polar opposites. Adeleine was smart and lively, while Nick was a bit childish and short sighted. Despite their differences, they seemed to make a perfect Yin-Yang of a couple. Adeleine would save Nick from slip ups during conversations and Nick would change the snow tires on Adeleine's car. It worked for them.

Nick and Adeleine make Opal think about her and Luca. How Luca used to be similar to Nick and how she wondered if they'd end up together. Opal always thought of herself as confident and tasteful while Luca grew into a man who was responsible and tactful.

Opal is brought out of her thoughts by Nick aggressively waving from the side entrance, as Adeleine makes her way back over to the table. Opal subtly waves back to Nick before he disappears through doors towards the kitchen, as Adeleine sits back down across from her.

"I didn't tell him, but he says you look nice today" Adeleine grins as she sips on her drink.

"Thank you" Opal grins softly.

The waitress comes back with their check, Adeleine insisting she pays before Opal obliges and sneaks a tip to the waitress behind Adeleine's back. The ride back home feels much longer than the one to the restaurant, but Opal enjoys it. Wondering what exactly she is going to be walking back into at home.

Chapter Ten

Opal arrives home to an empty house, feeling a bit relieved she decides to take a nap. Luca would probably be out all afternoon, seeing as the nearest airfield was two hours away. As she lays in bed on her phone, scrolling through endless photos she realizes tomorrow is Christmas Eve. Opal quickly sits up and grabs her laptop off of her nightstand and video calls her brother.

"Merry Early Christmas!" Two people on Opal's laptop screen exclaim.

"Merry Early Christmas!" Opal chirps back as she breaks into a wide grin.

Opal grew up in a three-person household. One adult and two children, her being one of the children. Her brother, Charlie, was always super protective of her. When Opal went to college in the United States, Charlie wanted to follow her across the Pacific Ocean but couldn't leave their mother behind. Despite this, their mother Isla had encouraged Charlie to go and explore. He would visit Opal but always ended up back home.

Isla raised Opal and Charlie in a tiny town on a large shore in Wales. Despite growing up in Great Britain, Opal never developed an accent. Opal attributed this to the fact that her and Charlie's father is an American man who grew up in New York City. Charlie, on the other hand, had a thick British accent you'd expect.

"How are you? Is Luca with you?" Charlie asks.

"He took Stephen to the airport to fly back home, you both have me all to yourselves" Opal smirks widely as she tilts her head.

"Well give him our love" Isla grins "How is his head injury? We spoke on the phone the other day and he seemed to be feeling better"

Opal dives into all of the details surrounding Luca's head injury. How he'd slipped and was seemingly stuck in two thousand and eleven for a couple weeks before he finally remembered everything. A fairly momentous moment despite Luca not fully telling Opal of his returned memories.

Isla comforts Opal, reminding her that while communication is key, so is patience. Once they finish discussing Luca, Charlie shows Opal sonograms of his little baby boy who is due any day now. Charlie talks about how excited he is, his face lighting up every time he talks about his unborn baby.

Opal finds herself over emotional and excuses herself for a moment as she heads downstairs to grab her purse. She pulls out a strip of her own sonograms, a tiny little speck of a bean resting in the middle of all the pictures. Opal shows Charlie and Isla and all three of them are reduced to sobbing.

"Opal…" Isla sniffles as she wipes her tear-stricken face "My baby is having a baby."

"As soon as little man comes, we're all going to fly out and see you and your little guy" Charlie grins before holding his hands up defensively "Or little lady!"

Opal tucks the sonograms away in the drawer of her nightstand before they all bid each other goodbye and end the call.

Opal slowly closes the lid to her laptop, a small smile on her lips as she leans back onto the plush comforter. Her eyelids heavy as she dozes off to sleep.

Meanwhile, Luca stands over a glass counter, his eyes landing on large diamond after diamond as he tries to figure out which ring Opal would like. He is very much aware that she likes her blue, rustic wedding band. Luca continues to skim while Stephen tries on watches at another counter.

It isn't until Luca feels like throwing his hands in the air that a small, circular aquamarine ring stands out to him. Luca points to it as the man behind the counter removes it from the glass for him to take a closer look at.

"It's Opal," Luca says softly.

"Actually, it's aquam-"

"I meant my wife" Luca chuckles, interrupting the man "Her name is Opal and this ring was practically made for her"

Stephen sets down the watch he had been admiring and claps Luca on the back.

"Dude" Stephen grins at the ring.

"I know, it'd match her wedding band perfectly" Luca smiles as he hands the ring back to the man "I'll take it."

Despite the high price tag, Luca takes a moment to go over which card is his wallet goes to what bank account. After a few moments, he turns back to the counter and hands the man a plastic card. He and Stephen grab a coffee from a nearby coffee shop before they get back on the road.

Two hours and a quick goodbye later, Luca finds himself back on the road. His heart skips a beat, thinking about how he is going to propose to Opal. The thought excites and terrifies him altogether at the same moment. By the time he's pulling into the garage, Luca knows exactly what his plan of action is. First, he just needs it to be Christmas Eve.

Luca enters the dark home slowly, wondering if Opal is even home. He tucks the ring away in a small drawer in the nightstand in the guest bedroom. He slowly makes his way upstairs, to find Opal asleep next to her half-closed laptop.

Luca shuts the laptop fully and sets it aside on Opal's nightstand. He lifts a throw blanket over her before leaning down and kissing her cheek. He can't help but notice something different about her. Something...softer. Luca knew he'd sound crazy if he tried to explain it, so he simply makes sure Opal is covered. He notices her nightstand drawer slightly open and pushes it closed all the way. His gaze washing over Opal one more time before he turns and quietly leaves the room.

Chapter Eleven

Opal rolls over to find a note from Luca on his pillow. Blinking quickly, Opal slowly sits up in bed. Stretching out her arms above her head before she rubs her eyes gently with her fingers. She reaches over to Luca's pillow and picks up the note, reading it silently to herself.

"Went out for a run, Merry Christmas Eve"

Opal sets the note back down, a content feeling in her gut as she gets up and walks into the bathroom. Completely prepared to begin her day, she slips into something comfortable. Opal heads downstairs to find the tree already lit up and the fire already crackling away.

A smile settles on her lips as she walks into the kitchen, pulling open different cabinets, the end result is a medley of utensils and ingredients to make pancakes. Blueberry pancakes, to be specific.

No matter how hard Opal tries to not burn the edges, she still does. Luca comes in through the back door a moment later, dressed head to toe in compression clothes. He smiles at Opal as he pulls off smaller items of clothing. His hat and gloves, he kicks his running shoes back outside before he wraps his arms around Opal.

His hands settle on her waist as he lifts her up onto the counter, Opal's slender fingers tangling up in Luca's hair. Opal settles into the kiss, momentarily forgetting about the pancakes before a burnt smell interrupts them, Opal gently nudging Luca as she hops off of the counter to shut off the stovetop.

"Well, on the upside" Opal smirks in Luca's direction "I have a stack ready to go"

Luca chuckles as she throws out the blackened pancake. Opal quickly submerges the pan in a sink full of soapy water, Luca sidling up next to her.

"Can I take you somewhere?" Luca whispers in Opal's ear.

Opal can feel the blush rising in her cheeks, her heart beating out of her chest as she turns to look at Luca.

"Yes"

Luca laces his fingers with Opal's and pulls her upstairs, both of them quickly changing clothes. Luca washing his face as Opal pins her hair back out of her face. As Opal walks towards the door, Luca suddenly pulls her back into his arms, his gaze on her as he gently bites his lip.

"I'm sorry for running out," Luca says so softly Opal almost doesn't hear him "I'm sorry if I hurt you, I would never intentionally hurt you"

"I know, you have nothing to apologize for"

"Are you sure?"

"I'm sure, I'm always sure when it comes to you"

Opal tilts her face closer to Luca's, their lips briefly meeting before Luca pulls back with a grin on his lips. He nudges his head towards the door, Opal nodding as both of them head downstairs. Luca leads Opal into the garage, opening the car door for her before climbing into the driver's seat.

"So, do I get to know where you are taking me?"

"Nope"

Luca pulls out of the driveway, pressing a button on a clicker attached to the car visor, the garage door closing as they driveaway. Opal reaches her hand across the console, her fingers finding Luca's once again as Luca drives through the small town of Bearsville.

Snow begins to fall lightly and the minutes turn into hours. The scenery continues to stay the same, the mountains for miles is where they resided, and Opal loved it. The curvature of the mountains, the way the snow would layer itself on each curve and contour. She loved when the fog rolled in after cold, rainy nights. The way the fog would flow down the mountains, blanketing all of the small towns.

Luca pulls into a gas station, Opal noticing they've been in the car for nearly four hours. Despite how much she is itching to ask him where they are going, the anticipation is also intriguing to her after the last few weeks they'd had. Luca returns with some munchies and soft drinks in hand, giving them to Opal through the window before he pumps gas into their car.

He climbs back in, Opal opening the crunchy cheese doodles first, Luca's favorite. Luca and Opal munch quietly as he continues driving to wherever their destination is. The sun begins to set all around them, Opal keeping track of the time.

They'd been in the car for seven hours.

Opal tries not to shift uncomfortably, but she has to pee, and her legs are starting to cramp. Luca turns off of the paved road and onto a gravel pathway, surrounded by more tall pine trees. After a moment, they reach a clearing with a small cabin all light up.

"Who lives here?" Opal asks as she takes in the sight in front of her.

"No one turns out I bought it before my accident, apparently it was a Christmas gift to you. You'll see why when we get inside" Luca smiles softly at Opal as he pulls to a stop in front of the small cabin.

Opal gets out as Luca pops the trunk and pulls out two duffel bags. He tosses Opal the keys to the cabin, so she can use the bathroom, while he brings the bags inside.

"Okay, when on earth did you have time to plan all of this?" Opal inquires, one of her eyebrows arched at Luca.

"I went through all of my stuff about a week ago. Bank statements and emails, everything" Luca says as he shuts the door behind him "I was planning this trip before the accident, I just happened to remember it before Christmas, so I had some time to pull it off"

"Luca, it's amazing" Opal smiles as she gestures around the cabin "But what about it am I supposed instantly fall in love with?"

Luca chuckles as he walks behind Opal and places his hands over her eyes. Luca leads her over to a large window on the back of the cabin, positioning her right in front of it before he moves his hands.

Opal slowly opens her eyes and gasps rather loudly, blinking back tears that threaten to ruin her view. In front of her is the most beautiful lake Opal had ever seen. She always through the view of the mountainside from their home was gorgeous, that mountainside had nothing on this lake.

"I can't wait to see it in the morning" Opal grins, her eyes never leaving the view of the lit-up lake "I should have brought my camera"

"I packed it"

Opal lets the tears fall down her face, nothing but pure euphoria flowing through her as she turns towards Luca and wraps her arms around his neck. She presses her tear stained lips to his, Luca sliding his hands around her waist, pulling her body closer to his until there is zero space between them.

"One more thing..." Luca says breathlessly as he slowly pulls back from the kiss.

Chapter Twelve

Despite how cold the air is, Opal follows Luca down a wooden staircase towards the lake. The air nips at little bits of revealed skin on Opal. She shivers a bit, Luca pulling her closer to him before they reach the gazebo. Luca helps her up onto the gazebo, the stairs nowhere to be found.

"I'll fix it" Luca laughs as Opal looks around.

The patio lights strung up around the gazebo, casting a soft glow on Luca and Opal. The top of the rundown gazebo has a gaping hole, causing Opal to temporarily gawk at it before Luca begins to play music. Opal turns her attention to a portable record player, where a slow song begins to play. It takes her a moment to realize it's not just any old slow song, it's the first song that was playing they heard after their shotgun wedding.

Luca holds his hand out, Opal placing her hand in his as they begin to sway to the music. Tears threatening to spill down her face again as they sway slowly back and forth. Opal rests her head on Luca's shoulder as he lets his cheek rest against the top of Opal's head. He presses a kiss to her forehead, Opal closing her eyes as she lets the music take over her. Her mind completely silent as she locks the memory playing out in front of her away in her mind. Never wanting to forget this moment.

The song comes to an end and as another song begins, Luca takes a shaky deep breath. Opal placing her hand gently against his cheek, a soft smile on her lips as Luca gets down on one knee.

"I want you to know, that I am aware that I do not deserve you. When I learned the other day that we had a shotgun wedding, something inside of me felt wrong. Like you were entitled to a proposal and I just didn't bother to go through with it" Luca pulls the small velvet box from his inner jacket pocket, slowly opening the box to reveal the small aquamarine ring "But I can promise you, that I will never stop loving you. If I fell and hit my head again, I would try just as hard to remember you and everything we had because it's worth remembering. You are worth remembering. You are more than my other half, my best friend. You are the light of my life and it would make me the happiest man alive, again, if you agreed to marry me all over again"

"Are you asking?" Opal chuckles as tears pool in her eyes.

"Opal, will you marry me?" Luca asks as he keeps his eyes on her.

"Yes" Opal nods "I would marry you again everyday if you asked"

Luca stands and pulls the ring from the box and slides it onto Opal's ring finger, the aquamarine ring sitting right above her wedding band, the colors dancing together on her finger perfectly. Luca tucks the small box away and lifts a small ribbon tied piece of mistletoe above Opal's head. Opal pulls her eyes away from her new ring to look up, a grin on her lips as she presses a kiss to Luca's lips.

"Will you drop that thing before you have an allergic reaction?" Opal whispers, knocking the mistletoe out of Luca's hand.

Luca let's it fall to the ground, both of his hands tugging Opal closer to him. Opal leans back a bit, her gaze on Luca as the moment finally seems right to her.

"I have something to tell you as well" Opal grins at him.

Luca arches his eyebrows at her. He lowers them, a small smile on his lips as he presses his forehead gently to hers,

"I'm pregnant"

Luca opens his eyes but keeps his forehead pressed to Opal's. He slowly kneels down in front of her, his knees pressing into the wood of the gazebo as he calmly unzips Opal's jacket, his fingers running around Opal's waist. He leans in closer and gently lifts up her sweater, his lips grazing her lower belly.

"Best Christmas *Ever*"

Author's Note:

Thank you so much for reading "Allergic to Mistletoe"! If you enjoyed the story or just want to give me some feedback, please feel free to shoot me an email (which can be found at my website, www.writingwithpaws.com) or find me on IG at @authorcveliz otherwise all feedback can be given through amazon.

That aside, a final thank you and I hope you have Happy Holiday's 2019!